This book is for students, teachers, and parents—
and everybody who looks forward to that first day of school.
TB

For students and teachers all over the world
JH

Text copyright © 2023 by Tom Brenner
Illustrations copyright © 2023 by Jen Hill

First edition 2023

Library of Congress Catalog Number 2021947121
ISBN 978-1-5362-0913-6

23 24 25 26 27 28 APS 10 9 8 7 6 5 4 3 2 1

Printed in Humen, Dongguan, China

This book was typeset in ITC Stone Informal.
The illustrations were done in mixed media.

Candlewick Press
99 Dover Street
Somerville, Massachusetts 02144

www.candlewick.com

And Then Comes SCHOOL

TOM BRENNER   illustrated by **JEN HILL**

CANDLEWICK PRESS

WHEN the days start off cool but get hot fast,
and the leaves of trees seem tired by noon,
and blackberries hang heavy on the vine . . .

THEN, with fingers stained deep purple, watch as the berries bob and boil into glistening jam.

WHEN the August sun turns
green lawns brown,
and neighbors linger in spots of shade,
and evening brings out the scritchy songs
of katydids and cicadas . . .

THEN race through the cool night air to play a game of flashlight tag.

WHEN pumpkins take on an orange tinge,
and the breeze carries the scent of ripening apples,
and tall sunflowers, full of seeds, begin to droop . . .

THEN bring in baskets
of flowers and fruits
and veggies.

WHEN a list of supplies arrives from school,
and Mom and Dad have sorted through your closet,
and outgrown clothes are ready to be passed on to someone smaller . . .

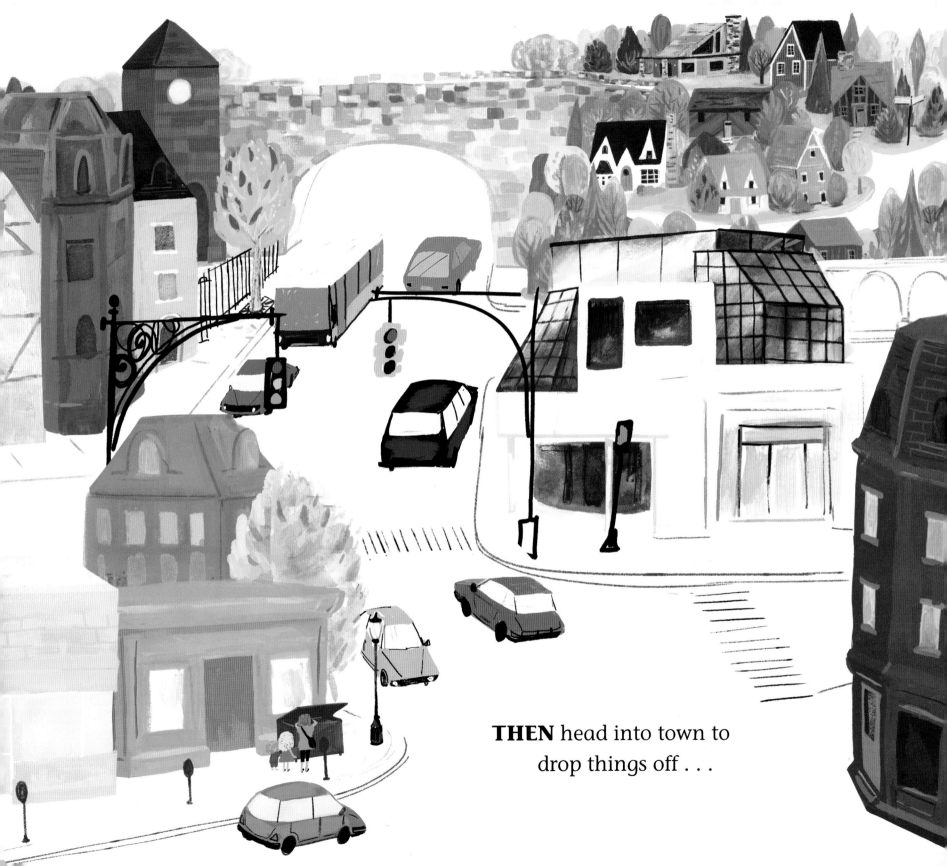

THEN head into town to
drop things off . . .

and pick things up!

WHEN the day before school finally arrives, and the air seems to buzz with excitement, and Mom and Dad have smiles for everything . . .

THEN run and play on this last day of vacation.

WHEN dinner is done
and your first-day outfit
has been decided,
and your new backpack
is stuffed with supplies,

and your lunch box is packed
with all your favorite things . . .

THEN slip into bed and imagine what tomorrow will bring.

WHEN the alarm clock rings out—
It's time! It's time! It's time!—
and the early-morning sky is the color of slate,
and the scent of syrup-soaked pancakes
drifts into your room . . .

THEN tuck into Dad's
extra-special breakfast,
put your lunch in your backpack . . .

and pose for a picture . . .

then another . . .

and another!

Skip to the end of the block,
climb aboard the waiting bus, filled with friends,
and wave till Mom and Dad disappear from view.

WHEN the bus pulls to a stop in front of the school,
and kids swirl around, all talking at once,
and everyone drifts toward the big front doors . . .

THEN hurry inside, where the sounds of bubbly chatter echo in the halls.

AND WHEN you find your new classroom,

and the smiling teacher says,
"Welcome! Come in! Come in!"
and a friend points to a desk
with your name on it . . .

THEN settle in for the start of the school day . . .
and a whole new year of learning.